LEVEL 2

LEGO

THE LEGO MOVIE 2

WELCOME TO APOCALYPSEBURG

Adapted by Kate Howard

SCHOLASTIC INC.

10 9 8 7 6 5 4 3 2 1   19 20 21 22 23
Printed in the U.S.A.   40

First printing 2019
Book design by Marissa Asuncion

In the days that followed, Bricksburg changed. The once great city was now a wasteland called Apocalypseburg.

Lucy had become an even stronger leader than before. She mastered the art of survival.

Unikitty was once a picture of happiness. After Taco Tuesday, she had no choice but to spend more time than ever as her alter ego: Angry Kitty.

And even though Batman was *always* awesome, no one could deny this new life had hardened everyone.

(Yes, even Batman.)

Well, it had hardened *almost* everyone. But not Emmet Brickowski. He was as cheerful and caring as always.

"Good morning!" Emmet would call out as he skipped through the streets of his favorite destroyed city. "Hello, Cyborgs. Hello, sewer babies!"

"Emmet," Lucy grumbled one morning. "You've got to stop pretending everything is awesome. It isn't."

"Oh no," Lucy moaned. "That's not a shooting star. It's something new . . ."

It was a spaceship!

As the spaceship drew closer, Emmet heard catchy music blasting out of the vessel. "That beat is pretty fresh!" Emmet said.

Suddenly, the ship launched a little heart-shaped device at the three friends.

"Hello!" the cute little heart said. Then it blinked and began to ring . . .

"RUN!" Lucy screamed.

Seconds later, the heart exploded. It blew everything around them into pieces.

Emmet and his friends fled in an escape vehicle that Lucy quickly built out of loose parts. But the strange space vessel tracked their every move.

When the spaceship found them, a masked pilot stepped out of it. She was the ship's general, and her name was Sweet Mayhem.

Sweet Mayhem ordered, "Bring me to your fiercest leader."

PERSONALITY ASSESSMENT

- WEAK
- NAIVE
- SIMPLE
- POWERLESS
- LESS THAN SPECIAL

Lucy pushed Emmet forward.

"*This* guy is a fierce warrior?" Sweet Mayhem asked.

Lucy shrugged. "Okay, well, *technically* I did the warrior stuff."

"You fought and master-built and then the hapless male was the leader?" Sweet Mayhem asked.

Sweet Mayhem shook her head. She was not impressed.

Before Emmet had a chance to defend himself, Sweet Mayhem gathered up all of Emmet's friends. She loaded them onto her ship and took them away!

"Lucy!" Emmet yelled as the ship blasted off. But his best friend was gone. Emmet was the only one who could get his friends back. He could finally *prove* he was a hero!

"Hang on to your fronds, Planty," Emmet said, preparing to launch into space. "We're going to save Lucy! And all the other people who were captured."

With nothing more than his pal Planty and a flying house rocket, Emmet blasted off into outer space to save his friends.

Meanwhile, Sweet Mayhem steered her prisoners toward their destination.

"Whoa!" Angry Kitty, Batman, Benny, and Metalbeard were all impressed by Sweet Mayhem's home.

"*Ahh!*" her friends continued.
"Stop it!" Lucy said.

In space, Emmet's ship was in danger! Luckily, help was nearby. "Mind if I save your life?" an ultra-cool space pilot asked. He swooped in to help steer Emmet's ship to safety.

THE NAME'S REX. REX DANGERVEST.

"I'm a big fan of yours," Rex told Emmet.
"You're the reason I started wearing a vest."
Rex joined Emmet on his mission!

Rex invited Emmet onto his ship.
It was crewed by a bunch of raptors!

As they blasted off into space, Emmet thought about all the fun times he and his best buds had together.

He needed to get them back. He *would* get them back.

It was time to make everything awesome again!